Runaway Molly Midnight
the artist's cat

Nadja Maril

Runaway
Molly Midnight
the artist's cat

with paintings and drawings
by Herman Maril

1980

Stemmer
House
PUBLISHERS, INC.

Owings Mills, Maryland

Inquiries should be directed to
Stemmer House Publishers, Inc.
2627 Caves Road
Owings Mills, Maryland, 21117

Published simultaneously in Canada
by Houghton Mifflin Canada Ltd., Markham, Ontario

A Barbara Holdridge book
Printed and bound in the United States of America

First Edition

Library of Congress Cataloging in Publication Data

Maril, Nadja.
    Runaway Molly Midnight, the artist's cat.

    SUMMARY: When a runaway cat returns to her home,
she discovers her human family has moved without her.
    [1. Cats—Fiction]   I. Maril, Herman.   II. Title.
PZ7.M3385Ru   [Fic]   80-17097
ISBN 916144-62-3
ISBN 0-916144-63-1 (pbk.)

To my husband Cyril

By the same author

Me, Molly Midnight, the Artist's Cat

I would like to give special thanks to the schoolchildren I have visited during the past two years, for their interest and desire to read more about the adventures of Molly Midnight.

I would also like to thank Adelyn Breeskin for her enthusiasm and support from the wings of the Smithsonian, my publisher Barbara Holdridge for her insightful criticism and guidance, my brother David for giving up part of his vacation to enable Molly to return home, and my parents Esta and Herman Maril for being themselves.

The story that follows is true.

I jumped up onto a window sill to get some air. The glass portion of the window had been opened and I pressed my nose against the screen to try and smell the flowers in the garden. I was always an indoor cat, but today I wanted to be outside. I watched two birds hopping about on the lawn. How I longed to chase after them until they finally had to beat their wings into the air and fly away. I pressed harder against the screen in my excitement, and it fell out of the window-frame. Here was my opportunity to go outside. All I had to do was jump through that open window. I could explore all those gardens, sand dunes and beaches, marshes and woods I'd seen in Herman's paintings.

Herman is an artist and I have been his favorite model for ever so long. My master, Herman, likes to tell everyone I'm fifteen years old. Fifteen years is not very old for a human being, but it is for a cat. His daughter, Suzanne, insists I'm only fourteen. She says she remembers that she was eleven years old when she first brought me home to live with her parents, Herman and Esta, and herself, here in Provincetown. Because Herman admired my sleek black fur and graceful lines, I was the focal point, you might say the star, of many of his paintings. There were "Me, Molly Midnight, sitting on a chair," "Me, Molly Midnight, stretched out on a rug".... (Of course, those were not the real titles of the paintings.) But now Herman has stopped painting pictures of me and he has started painting some watercolors instead. He says he doesn't want people to think he paints only cats.

I didn't even know at first what watercolors were, although I guessed that they had something to do with water. I did know that Herman loved to paint the sea in its many moods and colors. Were they water pictures?

Watching him work one day, I saw how he mixed his paints with water and used them to make sea

HERMAN MARIL

pictures. I had to admit I liked them, even if they did not include me. Looking at his watercolors, I could feel the wetness and peacefulness of the sea.

How I longed to be outside, to experience for myself the moods and feelings of Herman's paintings. Now, suddenly, I was free to explore the world I had gazed at. The painted out-of-doors looked so tempting—the green scrubby pines, the hot orange sand dunes, the dark green and blue ocean around

Provincetown. I could feel the sand beneath my paws. I jumped down to the ground outside the window. It was the terrace in front of the toolshed. The stone was rough and scratchy on my paws, but the air smelled wonderful. It was fresh and fragrant, and a gentle breeze blew against my fur.

A beautiful Monarch butterfly fluttered past me. I knew it was a Monarch because Suzanne had one, under pressed glass, that she had captured one summer at day camp. I recognized its orange wings with their black borders. I chased after it, running through Esta's flower garden. There were purple and pink petunias, white daisies, red and lavender zinnias and orange and yellow marigolds.

It was to the marigolds the Monarch kept returning again and again. I rushed to catch up with her. In my eagerness, I bent the flowers and got tangled up in their petals, but it was no use. She flew away.

Suzanne loved butterflies. She had drawn pictures of them all over her school papers and notebooks. Now I understood why. They were so light and free. That was why I had broken out of the house —so that I could be as free as the butterfly I was trying to chase.

I jumped up onto the stone wall dividing the house from the dirt road that ran beside it. Then I followed the dirt road back into the woods. The road

was sandy and dusty, and the air smelled of the pine trees growing on either side of it. They were the same scrubby pines I had seen in Herman's paintings.

There were only a few houses on the road. I heard the sound of human voices and began to run away from them. I saw a side path leading up a hill and scurried up it as fast as I could.

Then I noticed something moving in the bushes, long and thin and fast. It was green, almost the same shade of green as the moss. It wasn't easy to follow. I took small steps, trying not to make too much noise. What was it I was chasing? I was reminded of all those games I had played as a kitten, chasing the string around the living room. What had Suzanne called the string? . . . a snake, a make-believe snake. Only this one was real. Now I became scared. But while I was trying to decide whether or not to pounce on him (I couldn't remember whether real snakes bite or not), he lowered himself into a secret gully and I couldn't find him.

By this time it was starting to get dark, and I was beginning to feel hungry. Since I could find nothing to eat, I decided to go to sleep. Nearby there were some bushes where I felt I would be safe and protected. I crawled under them and curled myself up.

Drops of water falling on my fur awakened me the next morning and at first I was frightened.

"Why, it's raining," I told myself. "This must be what rain feels like. The thing to do is to find some shelter." I started running down towards the dirt road, and I found an old shack. I stood beside it, protected by the overhang of the roof.

Luckily the rain didn't last too long. The sun was shining. As soon as the waterdrops stopped falling, I scampered down to the end of the road.

There it was—a sand dune—just like the ones

I'd seen in Herman's paintings. It was huge. What a large mountain of sand! And right beside it were different colors of light coming down in an arch. What were those beautiful colors? They were like the colors reflected on the wall through the crystal hanging in Suzanne's window—blue and purple and green and yellow and orange and red. This must be a rainbow —a real rainbow!

I sat and watched the rainbow as long as it lasted. Then I walked onto the sand dune to see what it felt like to walk on a mountain of sand. But I could see I wasn't going to get very far. My paws kept sinking in the sand. I couldn't even climb to the top.

I was hungry for my breakfast. I turned around and started to look for some food. I didn't have very much practice as a huntress, so I decided that I would be better off looking for a house with people who would feed me.

Back off the dirt road I found a house well hidden by trees. No one appeared to be home. It had a large porch and right beside the door was a large dish of food. It was dog food! Now dog food is not one of my favorites, but that morning it tasted delicious.

I spent the next eight days exploring. I chased toads and caterpillars and field mice, but I never saw another rainbow. At night, when everyone else was asleep I would sneak back to the house with the dog food. Sometimes the dog would bark and frighten me.

Once in a while, I would think I heard someone in the woods calling my name—"Molly, Molly Midnight." But I didn't pay any attention to them. I was having my adventure and I wasn't going to cut it short. When I finally came home I was really going to be appreciated. And the longer I stayed away the more they would miss me.

One afternoon I was so hungry that I went up to the house with the dog food earlier than usual. I ate quickly and carefully, while listening for any sounds of an approaching dog. When I had almost eaten enough, I heard the sound of a car driving up the road. I ran to hide in the bushes. The car pulled up right beside the house. A man and a woman got out of the car. They were younger than Herman and Esta and older than Suzanne. They seemed to be arguing about something. The man slammed the car door hard.

I came out from under the bushes to try and cheer him up. That's what I do for Herman when he gets angry.

"Where did that cat come from?" he asked his wife.

"Go home, kitty," he told me. I didn't understand why he wanted me to leave.

His wife's eyes opened wide. She was frightened of me. "A black cat," she exclaimed. "Get it out of here. Don't let it cross my path."

"Go home, blackie," her husband repeated.

I meowed innocently, delighting in the havoc I was causing. The woman went into the house and came out with a broom. What was the broom for? I wondered. Were they going to play a game with me?

"Shoo cat, shoo!" The woman came towards me, thrusting the broom in my face. I looked at her black, pointed shoes and the broom returning to hit me once more and I turned around and ran as fast as my legs could carry me into the woods.

The only place I knew I'd feel safe was home with my family. I ran down the dirt road towards their house. They would never hit me with a broom, I knew. I squeezed under the hedges and into Esta's garden. There was no car in the driveway and the gate was closed. The house was quiet. There was nobody home to greet me and it made me very angry. I went to the front door and meowed plaintively. No one was home to let me in. I felt all alone.

Just then a car drove up. Out of it walked David, Suzanne's older brother, who doesn't like me at all.

"What are you doing here?" he asked me when he reached the front door. "Why didn't you come home yesterday, you dumb cat?"

Yesterday? Why yesterday?, I asked myself. He let me into the house and there was no sign of the rest of the family. Everything seemed empty and bare. Why, they had returned to the city without me!

David went over to the phone and dialed a number. "Hello, Mom . . . guess who showed up a day late . . . Molly."

I could tell he was angry. How were they going to get me back to Baltimore? David lived in Massachusetts. He was a sports editor for a newspaper. He didn't have time to bother with cats, I heard him tell his mother. "As long as she stays with me she gets dry cat food. If that cat could survive on her own for ten days outside, she can survive on dry cat food for a while." I could hear Esta's voice on the phone and I could tell that she wasn't too happy about this. Neither was I.

But the next day David put me in a wooden box with only a screen for me to look through. Next, he tied a heavy rope around it and took me into his car. We drove for hours until we arrived at a big noisy place. I could feel strong vibrations in the air. I couldn't see much, but I could sense a lot of cars and people. He handed me—box and all—to a man behind the counter in one of the buildings.

"Is this the Freight Department?" I heard him ask. "I have one cat, named Molly Midnight, going to the Baltimore-Washington Airport."

An airport! So that's where I was. I had heard of airplanes—big machines with wings that flew in the air above the birds and even the clouds. This was going to be exciting.

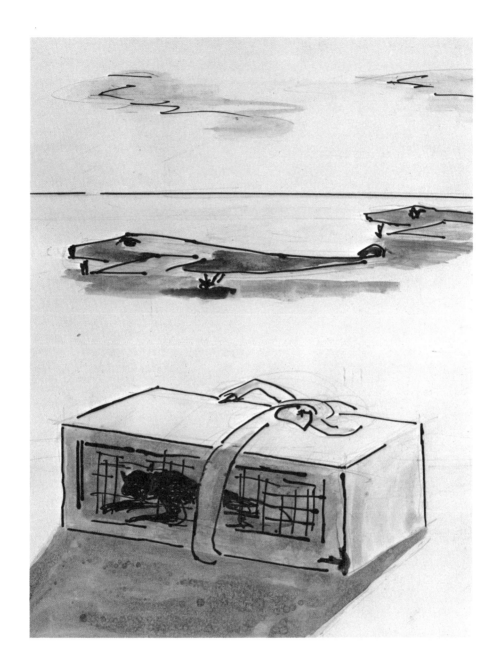

I crouched in my box and purred as the strange man carried me outside and lifted me onto a big platform with wheels. Another man wheeled the platform to the plane. The plane was gigantic. He lifted me into a dark place which was low and stuffy. I couldn't see anything. How was I going to see the tops of the trees and clouds?

A few minutes later I began to feel the vibrations of the engine getting ready for the takeoff. The plane began to move just like a car. Then my stomach began to churn and feel uneasy and I knew we were leaving the ground. I could feel the plane rising higher and higher. I must have been high above the clouds. I dreamed of gliding right through them.

My dream turned into a nightmare . . . I felt I was falling—falling. I awoke with a jolt. The plane had landed.

Another stranger took my box down out of the plane, looked into it and laughed. What was he laughing about? There was nothing funny about me! He took me into another big building, and I lay in my box, waiting.

"Well, your owners have come for you, Molly." Another man picked up my box and handed it to Esta and Suzanne.

"Well, thank goodness," I said to myself.

"Molly, did you have a good trip?" Esta asked me.

I began to meow and meow. "It was terrible," I was telling her. "I didn't see anything, and I'm so hungry."

"Don't worry," she told me. "We'll be home soon."

"Well, Molly," said Suzanne, "you had your first plane ride. I think you stayed away longer on purpose—just so you could fly home."

"That's what you think," I thought.

"Meow," I cried, when they got me into the house.

"Why, she looks like a prisoner," Herman said, "with that heavy rope wrapped around her box.

"Molly, I'm not having anything to do with you," he told me. "You hurt my feelings, running away from home like that. I worried about you."

I pretended not to care about what he had said. I ran into the kitchen to get something to eat. After I had eaten as much as I could, I lay back and looked at the furniture and paintings. I looked at Esta and Herman. I loved them. I even loved Suzanne. I didn't mean to hurt them. I just wanted an adventure.

Now that I was home, all my efforts to have an exciting adventure didn't seem so important. What I wanted now was to be petted and talked to. While I was away in the woods I had been all alone. Suppose Herman decided to ignore me for the rest of my life.

I went over to his feet and rubbed against his legs.

"You know I can't stay angry with you for long, Molly," he told me. "You've gotten so thin and sleek, I'll have to put you in another painting."

I got up on his lap and purred. Now, that was what I wanted to hear. He loved me, I knew. But now I knew more about him too. Now when I looked at his paintings I could remember the feelings I had had out-of-doors. I knew that Herman must have those feelings too, in order to paint the trees and the fields and the water the way he does. The paintings would always help me to remember the way I had felt. Maybe that was why Herman painted. It was a way to capture his feelings. And when I thought about it, it no longer bothered me not to be in every one of Herman's pictures. I could put myself in them anytime I wanted to, just by looking at them and remembering the way it had been.

"I'm content to stay at home now," I told him.

He smiled and said, "Why should you want to run away from home when you have everything you need right here?"

I knew he was right, but I had to find out for myself.

Paintings by Herman Maril in this book

Runaway Molly Midnight, the Artist's Cat
Composed by the Service Composition Company, Baltimore, Maryland
   in Century Expanded with Torino Roman Swash display
Color separation by Capper, Inc., Knoxville, Tennessee
Printed by A. Hoen & Co., Baltimore, Maryland
   on white Old Forge Opaque, Regular Finish
Bound in paper by Bindagraphics, Inc., Baltimore, Maryland
Hardbound in Kivar 5 Wedgewood, Linenweave, by Delmar
   Printing Company, Charlotte, North Carolina